Dear Parents,

The easy-to-read books in this series are based on The Puzzle Place™, public television's highly praised new show for children that teaches not ABC's or 123's, but "human being" lessons!

In these books, your child will learn about getting along with children from all different backgrounds, about dealing with problems, and about making decisions—even when the best thing to do is not always so clear.

Filled with humor, the stories are about situations that all kids face. And best of all, kids can read them all on their own, building a sense of independence and pride.

So come along to the place where it all happens. Come along to The Puzzle Place™....

ISBN 0-448-41299-3   A B C D E F G H I J

The Puzzle Place™ is a co-production of Lancit Media Productions, Ltd., and KCET/Los Angeles. Major funding
provided by the Corporation for Public Broadcasting and Edison International.

OH, THAT NUZZLE!

By David Johnson

Illustrated by Tom Brannon

GROSSET & DUNLAP · NEW YORK

Nuzzle and Sizzle
are having a race
all around
The Puzzle Place.

Suddenly Nuzzle says that he
is just as hungry as can be.

"Oh, look!" he says.
"What do I see?
    Some tasty cookies!
    Lucky me!"

He eats the cookies—
one, two, three.

Sizzle waits until he's done.

"All gone!" she says.

"Let's have some fun."

But Nuzzle does not
want to play.
He sees some pancakes
on a tray.

He takes a bite
and says, "Yum, yum!"
Then Nuzzle eats up
every crumb.

Sizzle sees what Nuzzle does.

She says,

"You're eating too much, Nuz."

But Nuzzle cannot
stop himself.
He sees dog biscuits
on a shelf.

"I think you should not
eat that stuff,"
says Sizzle.
"You have had enough."

Sizzle pulls
with all her might.
But Nuzzle says,
"Just one more bite!"

He has some cheese
on a roll.

He has some noodles
in a bowl.

He has some pie.

He has some cake.

And soon he has...

...a tummy ache!

He says,

"I made a big mistake!"

"Poor Nuzzle!"
Sizzle says with woe.
She does not say,
"I told you so."

She brings her friend
a cup of tea.
She is as helpful
as can be.

Nuzzle says,
"I will not eat
another pie,
another treat.
No doggie biscuits
will I chew.
Not even three.
Not even two."

"Not even two.
Not even one.
Not even one
just for fun!"